NOAH WILD
AND THE
FLOATING ZOO

NOAH WILD
AND THE
FLOATING ZOO

ALEXANDER McCALL SMITH

ILLUSTRATED BY NICOLA KINNEAR

BLOOMSBURY
CHILDREN'S BOOKS
LONDON OXFORD NEW YORK NEW DELHI SYDNEY

BLOOMSBURY CHILDREN'S BOOKS
Bloomsbury Publishing Plc
50 Bedford Square, London WC1B 3DP, UK
29 Earlsfort Terrace, Dublin 2, Ireland

BLOOMSBURY, BLOOMSBURY CHILDREN'S BOOKS and the Diana logo
are trademarks of Bloomsbury Publishing Plc

First published in Great Britain in 2020 by Bloomsbury Publishing Plc
This edition published in Great Britain in 2021 by Bloomsbury Publishing Plc

A catalogue record for this book is available from the British Library

ISBN: PB: 978-1-5266-0555-9; eBook: 978-1-5266-0552-8

2 4 6 8 10 9 7 5 3 1

Typeset by RefineCatch Limited, Bungay, Suffolk
Printed and bound in Great Britain by CPI Group (UK) Ltd, Croydon CR0 4YY

To find out more about our authors and books visit www.bloomsbury.com
and sign up for our newsletters

This is for Douglas Mant

~ 1 ~

This is the story of a boy called Noah Wild and his sister, Hatty Wild. They were very good friends, as well as being brother and sister, and they lived with their aunt, whom they called Aunt Smiley. Nobody can remember why they called her that, but the name seemed to suit her, as Aunt Smiley was a smiley sort of person, who was happy to allow Noah and Hatty to do more or less as they

pleased, as long as they behaved themselves, were polite, washed their hands
before meals, and kept their bedrooms
tidy or tidy-ish, which is not quite the
same as tidy.

Their parents were both famous moun-
taineers, who spent much of their time
climbing high mountains in distant countries. That was their job, and they needed
to do it to earn money for the family
to live on. Sometimes people have to
do that – they would much prefer to be
at home, but they have to go to work
somewhere else. The Wilds took people
up mountains and then brought them
down again. They did not get paid very

much for this, but they still sent any spare money they had back home to provide for Noah and Hatty. And they wrote to them regularly too, sending them long letters with pictures of the mountains they had climbed.

Aunt Smiley was kind to the children. She was good at most things, especially knitting, and she knitted all their winter jumpers out of red and yellow wool. In the summer, she made them clothes out of canvas, cut from old tents. These clothes were much cooler, as well as being much brighter and more comfortable than anything you could buy in shops. And it saved money too, which could then be spent on food and outings to the cinema, with large buckets of popcorn. They were all very happy.

"I really like Aunt Smiley," Noah often said to his sister. "She must be the kindest aunt in the whole world."

"Very probably she is," said Hatty, who agreed with most things her brother said, just as he agreed with most things she said.

As well as their aunt, Noah and Hatty had an uncle, Loafy Wild. He was a ship's captain by trade, but he was called Loafy because he was also a very good baker. He made loaves of bread in all sorts of sizes and shapes, and everyone said that there was no more delicious bread than his in the whole country.

Rather like Aunt Smiley, Uncle Loafy smiled a lot. He also had a deep laugh that sounded a bit like a drain gurgling. And another thing about him was that he had only one leg – or only one leg that was his own, the other being an artificial leg made of cork.

"If I ever fall in the sea," Uncle Loafy

joked, "I will float very easily because of my cork leg."

Hatty and Noah had been told how Uncle Loafy lost his leg. It was all to do with something that happened at sea, Aunt Smiley explained. "He fell overboard some years ago," she said. "A shark got him, I'm afraid. Well, it got a bit of him!"

Noah winced. "That's very bad luck," he said.

"Yes," said Aunt Smiley. "But they fitted him with his cork leg and he gets about just fine. And you know what? Loafy never complained – not once. In fact, he said, 'I think I'm really lucky that the shark didn't bite off both my legs.' Now, that's what I call being positive."

Uncle Loafy was a ship's captain and a baker, but that was not all. "Did you know that your Uncle Loafy owns a zoo?" Aunt Smiley said one day.

"A zoo!" exclaimed Hatty.

"Yes," Aunt Smiley went on. "You see, one day Loafy met a man who gave him a zoo. It seems that the man had to go off to Australia to live with his son and daughter, and needed to find somebody to take a zoo off his hands. He gave it to your Uncle Loafy."

Noah whistled. "Wow! A zoo. And what happened then?"

"Well, because Loafy was off at sea a great deal," Aunt Smiley continued, "he had to get a friend to run the zoo for him. He had a friend called Roger Porridge, and Roger became the head zookeeper."

Noah looked at Hatty. "Imagine having a zoo," he said.

Hatty shook her head. "I'd love to meet some of his animals," she said. "Wouldn't you?"

Noah thought for a moment. Then he replied, "Yes, I think I would."

He did not know, of course, what was going to happen only three days later. I imagine that you've already guessed, but let's see.

Exactly three days later, Aunt Smiley announced that there had been a telephone call from Uncle Loafy.

"Uncle Loafy is coming for tea this afternoon," she said. "His ship has just returned from a trip to Jamaica to collect a cargo of bananas. He will be here later today."

Uncle Loafy arrived at exactly four o'clock in a very old red car with three wheels – one at the front and two at the back. As he climbed out of the driver's seat, the first thing he said to Noah and

Hatty was, "How many wheels does my
car have, my dears?"

"Three," said Noah, and added, "Most
cars have four, Uncle Loafy."

"That's right," said Uncle Loafy. "I used
to have four, but I lost one, I'm afraid.
It's a long story and I'll tell you more
about it when we have more time. Now

what I want is some tea and cake." He smiled at Hatty. "I take it you like cake, Hatty."

Hatty nodded. "I like it very much, Uncle Loafy."

"Well, in that case," said Uncle Loafy, "if you look in the back of the car there, you'll find several large boxes. Do me a favour, please, and bring them inside."

Hatty did as she was told. But as she opened the door of the car and peered inside, she gave loud shriek of surprise.

"There's a monkey in there," she shouted.

Uncle Loafy laughed. "Oh, yes!" he said. "Of course, there's a monkey. That's

Monkey Robertson. I forgot all about him, but I think he'll want to come in for tea. He always likes to see what's going on."

No sooner had he said this than a monkey scampered out of the car and jumped up on Uncle Loafy's shoulder.

"He loves to ride on my shoulder," said Uncle Loafy. And then he said to Hatty, "Don't forget the boxes of cake."

Hatty reached into the car. The boxes were rather heavy, and had the most delicious smell coming out of them. It was a smell made up of icing sugar and strawberries, of several sorts of chocolate, and of marzipan. It was a very promising smell.

Aunt Smiley gave her brother a hug at the front door and they all went into the kitchen, where places had been laid for tea. The cakes were soon taken out of the boxes and placed in full view on the table. Hatty had never seen so many cakes in her life, and none as delicious-looking as this. Uncle Loafy smiled as he suggested she and Noah put a couple of cakes on everybody's plate.

"And don't forget Monkey Robertson," he said. "He's particularly partial to a spot of cake."

They sat down at the table. Monkey Robertson sat on Uncle Loafy's shoulder, but every so often he hopped on to the

13

table and helped himself to a piece of cake, scattering crumbs all around as he did so. He did not have very good table manners, thought Noah, but then he *was* a monkey, and you can't expect too much of a monkey.

"While we're eating," Uncle Loafy said, "I shall give you some very important news. Are you listening attentively?"

Noah and Hatty nodded. They thought their uncle was amazing, and they could barely wait to hear what he had to say.

"Now then," Uncle Loafy began. "You may have heard that some years ago I was given a zoo."

"Aunt Smiley told us that," said Noah.

"Did she, then?" Uncle Loafy continued. "Well, she was correct. I was given this zoo, you see, but I couldn't really look after it myself. So I asked my friend …"

"Roger Porridge?" prompted Noah.

"Precisely," said Uncle Loafy. "Roger and I go back a long way. We were friends as boys, and we've remained friends since then. Roger has always been rather good with animals, and so I asked him to look after my zoo for me." He paused, and helped himself to another cake.

"He is an extremely good zookeeper, is Roger," Uncle Loafy continued. "But now he says he wants to retire. He has bought a little plot of land and he wants to grow carrots and asparagus. Which is a perfectly reasonable thing to want to do."

"I can quite understand," said Aunt Smiley. "Looking after a zoo must be hard work."

"It is," said Uncle Loafy. "But where does that leave me? More precisely, where does it leave my zoo?"

"Could you not find somebody else?" asked Noah.

Uncle Loafy sighed. "I've tried. But unfortunately there doesn't seem to be anybody who can do the job." He sighed again. "And I'm afraid I'm not much use with animals, to tell the truth. I like them, of course, but I don't really know much about looking after them."

Noah and Hatty were silent. It seemed an awful pity to have a zoo but not to have anybody to look after it.

"And so," Uncle Loafy continued, "I made up my mind. I've sold most of the animals to another zoo. They are being looked after very well in their new home, but they didn't want to take all of them. And so I have four animals left."

"Only four?" asked Hatty. "Which ones are they?"

Uncle Loafy reached out for a fourth piece of cake. "Delicious cake, this," he said. "Which animals are left, you ask? I'll tell you. I have a South American llama, a kangaroo, an Indian tiger and, of course, our friend Monkey Robertson. He comes from Africa, I believe. You'll know where the kangaroo comes from, I expect. And the Indian tiger comes from …"

"India," said Noah.

"You're a smart boy," said Uncle Loafy. "Have another cake."

Uncle Loafy told them a bit more about the animals. "They each have a name," he said. "The llama is called Henrietta and the kangaroo is called Mrs Roo."

Noah said that he thought those were very good names for a llama and a kangaroo.

"Thank you," said Uncle Loafy. "And the tiger is called Ram. I'm afraid he's terribly fierce, but I suppose that's what you must expect of a tiger."

Hatty asked him what he was going to do with them.

Uncle Loafy did not hesitate. "I'm going to return them, of course," he said. "They're going home."

"To South America and Australia?" asked Noah.

"And to India?" Hatty enquired.

"Yes," said Uncle Loafy.

Noah was watching Monkey Robertson, who was licking cake icing off his tiny monkey fingers. "And what about him?" he asked, nodding towards Monkey Robertson.

"I'll take him home too," he said. "Back to Africa."

Noah knew that monkeys cannot understand what people say, but it seemed to him that Monkey Robertson was following this conversation and had shaken his head when it was suggested he go back to Africa. He did not have time to mention this, though, as Uncle Loafy had something else to say.

"You know that I have a boat?" he announced.

"Yes," said Noah. "I've seen a picture of it."

"That's the one," said Uncle Loafy. "Well, I have a boat, and I have charts — those are maps of the sea — that tell me how to get to these places, but ..." He looked at Aunt Smiley. "I don't have a crew, and I need at least two people to help me sail the boat and take the animals home."

There was silence. Noah and Hatty had both seen where this was going. They both hardly dared hope. They would do it — oh yes, they would do it as quick as a flash. But would Aunt Smiley let them go off on a dangerous voyage to the four corners of the earth in her brother's old boat? Aunts can be funny about that sort of thing.

Uncle Loafy now spoke directly to Aunt Smiley. "You don't happen to know two people who would like to help?" he asked.

The silence returned. Then Aunt Smiley said, "Well, there's Noah and Hatty, of course. They both like animals."

Uncle Loafy slapped his cork leg with pleasure. "The very people I was thinking of," he said.

"And then," Aunt Smiley continued, "I have a bit of time on my hands too. So, why don't we all go? You, me, Noah and Hatty. All four of us."

"Four is a very good number," said Uncle Loafy, helping himself to a final cake.

~ 2 ~

There was a great deal to do before they could set off. Uncle Loafy busied himself with the boat, helped by Hatty, who was very good at woodwork.

"I seem to have picked up a few holes," he said. "Holes in a boat can be a bit of a problem. You know that, I imagine, Hatty."

Hatty nodded. She had already had a good look round the boat and realised that it needed a lot of fixing.

"My poor old boat had a proper name, once," Uncle Loafy explained. "But I forgot it a long time ago. So these days she's just known as *The Ark*. That's a good name, don't you think?"

Hatty agreed. *The Ark* was a comfortable name, and Uncle Loafy's boat was a comfortable boat, for all that it had holes in it.

"We can fix the holes," Uncle Loafy said, pointing to a stack of round wooden pegs laid out on the deck. "You stick those pegs in the holes and then you chop off the extra bits. And then you're good as new."

Monkey Robertson was watching as Uncle Loafy showed Hatty how to fix the holes. Helping himself to some of the pegs, he tried to fit them into holes but was not very good at it.

"You can watch," Uncle Loafy scolded him, taking back the pegs Monkey Robertson had taken. "This is not a job for monkeys."

Hatty had soon mastered the task, helping Uncle Loafy hammer the wooden plugs into position. Then, each armed with a saw, they would trim the wood so as to create a perfect filling. They made good progress, and soon they had knocked the last peg into position and neatly trimmed it off. Behind them, though, Monkey Robertson had been pulling some of the pegs out of their holes and putting them into other holes. He seemed very proud of his handiwork when Hatty discovered what he had been doing, and was very upset that she disapproved.

"We're going to have to do it all over again," she said, shaking a finger at him. "I know you mean well, but this really is no help at all, Monkey Robertson."

It took some time to undo the mischief that Monkey Robertson had done, and it was only then that they could attend to the engine, which had been making a very strange wheezing sound.

"When an engine has a cough," said Uncle Loafy, "it means that it needs fixing."

While they were doing this, Noah and Aunt Smiley were drawing up lists of food they would need for the voyage.

"It depends on how long we're going to be away," said Aunt Smiley. "Did Uncle Loafy tell you?"

Noah shook his head. "He just said it would be a long time."

"Months and months, then," Aunt Smiley concluded. "Which means we shall need a lot of food, Noah."

They began to buy the supplies. There were one hundred packets of flour for baking bread – and the occasional cake. There was a whole ton of potatoes. There were three hundred and forty-eight tins of spinach. And that was just to start. There were many other supplies that had to be ordered, unpacked and then stowed away in the hold of *The Ark*.

Monkey Robertson was watching. He was very interested in food and thought it would be a good idea if he sampled some of the supplies that Noah and Aunt Smiley had brought on board. Looking about him to be sure that nobody was watching, Monkey Robertson opened various jars and stuck his fingers inside to taste the contents. He took out preserved plums and tasted them before putting them back in their jar; he scattered raisins on the floor and then picked them up, one by one, and popped them into his mouth; he stuffed olives into packets of sugar, and

sprinkled sugar over tomatoes. He made an awful mess before he was eventually discovered.

Aunt Smiley scolded Monkey Robertson loudly and shooed him out of the store-room. "That monkey!" she muttered. "That monkey is nothing but trouble!"

Noah saw what she meant, but he had to smile. He liked Monkey Robertson, and thought that, even if he did cause a lot of trouble, he would be fun to have around. And Monkey Robertson, he felt, liked him, as he kept leaping on to his shoulders, placing a paw on his head, and looking very proud of his friend. And the monkey also kept fetching him bananas, offering them as a present, even when Noah was not at all hungry.

Now it was time to arrange accommodation for the animals.

"We can't put them all together," said Uncle Loafy. "You can't put an Indian tiger in with a llama because …"

"Because the tiger would eat the llama?" asked Noah.

Uncle Loafy nodded. "Ram would eat anything," he said, "including us, if we weren't careful."

Noah was worried. He did not like the thought of being eaten by an Indian tiger — or by anything, for that matter.

"Not that he'll have the chance," Uncle Loafy continued quickly. "And, actually, he's not a bad tiger, that one. He'd only eat you if he was very, very hungry."

"I see," said Noah. But he was still a bit concerned.

"And anyway," Uncle Loafy went on, "the other animals don't like sharing cages. Nobody likes having Monkey Robertson jumping around at all hours of the day, playing tricks. How can Henrietta get some sleep if a monkey is pulling her tail? Llamas don't like that sort of thing. And how does Mrs Roo get her fair share of grass if Henrietta has nibbled it all up?"

There was only one thing for it, and

that was to build new quarters for each of the animals, and Uncle Loafy and Hatty set to this task after they had finished with the engine. Soon there were four bright new cages on the deck, each with a sleeping area and a thick bedding of straw. Each had a door through which the animal could pass freely – except for the tiger's cage, which was kept locked. "We don't want a tiger wandering about *The Ark*, do we?" asked Uncle Loafy.

"No," said Hatty. "I don't think we do."

Shortly after they had finished their work on the cages, the last of the supplies were loaded and Aunt Smiley was able to report to Uncle Loafy that as far as she was concerned, *The Ark* was ready to sail.

"In that case," said Uncle Loafy. "I shall go and fetch the other animals. They're very excited because they can sense that something's going to happen."

Noah and Hatty went with him to help, and after about twenty minutes they all returned with a trailer behind them. The trailer was stacked with three travelling cages of varying sizes, and in each of these was one of the three remaining animals. They were soon settled in on deck and Uncle Loafy was able to enquire whether everybody was absolutely ready.

"All present and correct, Captain!" answered Aunt Smiley. She had bought herself a sailor's outfit and was quickly picking up all the nautical words.

"Then let's put to sea," said Uncle Loafy. "I shall take the helm while Hatty and Noah operate the ship's horn."

Operating the ship's horn was exactly what Noah had been longing to do. Now he was able to pull on the cord that sounded the great bellowing blast of the horn, warning any other ships in the sea nearby of the presence of *The Ark*. On the deck, the sound of the horn excited the animals. Ram the tiger gave a great roar; Henrietta the llama lifted up her head and whinnied; Monkey Robertson shrieked; and Mrs Roo made a sort of sniffing sound that sounded like a rabbit blowing its nose.

Noah and Hatty looked back at the receding shore. It was a treat to be on Uncle Loafy's ship, and it was also a thrill to be taking the animals home, but at the same time the great ocean lay before them and there were bound to be hidden dangers to contend with.

"Are you frightened?" Hatty asked her brother. "Just a tiny bit frightened?"

Noah swallowed hard. He was about to say no when he checked himself and said yes, instead. But then he added, "Not too much, though. I am frightened, but only a tiny bit." He turned to his sister and

smiled. "I know that you'll have fixed those holes pretty well."

She smiled and thanked him. "Uncle Loafy says that we're heading for South America first," she said.

Noah was pleased to hear that. He had read about the Amazon and the mountains of the Andes. They would set Henrietta free in the Andes, Uncle Loafy had told them. "There's nothing that a llama likes more than to be up in the Andes," he said.

"I'm sure she'll be very happy," said Noah.

It took a long time. After stopping at a group of islands to take on more fuel, *The*

Ark pointed her nose at South America and set off across the wide blue fields of ocean. Day followed day as the ship ploughed through the waves. Now and then there was something interesting to see – a whale, perhaps, throwing up a spout of water in the distance, or flying fish, skimming across the surface of the water, sometimes landing with a plop on the deck of *The Ark*. For most of the time, though, there was nothing but sea, and then more sea.

It was Monkey Robertson who first sighted land. He had been swinging on a rope tied to the top of the mast, and this gave him a good view of what lay ahead. Suddenly he started to squeal, pointing excitedly towards the horizon.

"Monkey Robertson's seen something!" shouted Noah.

"Climb up and take a look," replied Uncle Loafy from the helm.

Noah and Hatty climbed up the mast and peered in the direction in which Monkey Robertson had been pointing. At first Noah thought that he was imagining things, but then a tiny smudge on the horizon grew higher and thicker.

"Land ahoy!" he shouted.

Everyone rushed up on deck. Uncle Loafy raised his telescope to his right eye. "That's South America," he said. "Well spotted, Noah."

From the cages on the deck there came a soft winnowing sound. Hatty turned round and saw Henrietta standing bolt upright, her nostrils flared, her eyes shining bright.

"She's seen it," Hatty whispered to Noah. "She's seen her home."

~ 3 ~

U ncle Loafy had skilfully navigated *The Ark* so that they would arrive in a mountainous part of South America. There was a harbour, of course, and a bit of flat land behind that, but there, in the distance, rising up to meet the sky, was a great range of mountains.

"Those are the Andes," he said, after they had safely docked *The Ark* in the harbour.

"They look terribly high," said Hatty. "Will we have to go right to the top?"

Uncle Loafy shook his head. "No," he said. "It's just snow and ice up at the very top. We'll only go about halfway up – but that's still quite high enough."

They made their preparations, and the next day they all set off, walking in a long line. Uncle Loafy was at the front, and he was followed by Hatty and then by Noah, who was leading Henrietta on a rein. Finally, bringing up the rear, was Aunt Smiley, who was wearing special fur-lined mountain boots and carrying an ice axe – just in case.

Henrietta was still excited, and was

sniffing at the breeze with the air of a creature picking up just the right scents. She did not have to be encouraged to walk; quite the opposite, in fact, as Noah had to struggle to stop her from rushing off headlong in the direction of the mountains.

They walked for most of the morning and at last found themselves halfway up a mountain. They had been following a stony mountain track, and now they sat down beside it and took out the picnic that Aunt Smiley and Noah had prepared back on *The Ark*. They had not forgotten about Henrietta, who was offered a special bag of lettuce leaves and bean shoots for her lunch. She ate that with great enjoyment, although Noah could tell that she was keen to get back on the track as soon as possible.

After the picnic, they resumed their journey. Being more than halfway up, they found that the air was getting much colder, and there were scattered drifts of snow here and there. At last, when they were a bit further up the mountain, they found a place to set up camp. Uncle Loafy had packed four tents, each of them big enough for just one person. These were pitched in a circle near the track and a campfire was built in the middle. Henrietta was tethered to a stake driven into the ground and was happy enough there, as there was some sweet green grass growing nearby and she could just reach it from the end of her tether.

Darkness fell. The mountain air was cold and the sky was a great velvet bowl studded with stars. With the fire to warm them, they ate their supper of stew and fried bananas in syrup. Then, everybody crawled into their tents, zipped themselves into their sleeping bags, and drifted off to sleep. There was a lot to do the next day, as that would be when they hoped to find a herd of wild llamas to which Henrietta could be introduced. This, they hoped, would be her new family. They would then say goodbye and make their way back to *The Ark*, where the other animals were waiting for their own chance of freedom.

When morning came it did not take them long to find a new family for Henrietta.

As the sun came up over the high peaks of the Andes, Noah saw a herd of wild llamas grazing on a nearby slope.

"Over there!" he shouted to Uncle Loafy. "Llamas!"

Uncle Loafy untethered Henrietta and clapped his hands to drive her towards her new friends. She did not take much persuading, and cantered off towards the herd, ears pricked up in excitement.

"She's so happy," said Hatty. "She loves being home."

"Yes," agreed Aunt Smiley. "She's very …"

She was about to say that the llama was very happy, but she stopped mid-sentence.

Henrietta was not happy at all. As she approached the herd, one of its members stepped forward to meet her. This llama, which was at least twice the size of Henrietta, seemed to be challenging her.

"They're suspicious," said Noah. "But I'm sure they'll get to know her."

Aunt Smiley was not so sure. "I hope she's all right," she said. "She's a very gentle llama and that bunch of llamas look anything but friendly."

Aunt Smiley was right. The llamas were not looking at all pleased to see a new member of their herd, and within a very few minutes Henrietta came scuttling back, looking most unhappy.

"Why are they being so nasty to her?" asked Noah. "What have they got against her?"

Uncle Loafy tried to shoo Henrietta back to the herd. He flapped his arms at her, and stamped his feet, but Henrietta shook her head stubbornly.

It was at this point that a boy riding a donkey came up the path. As he drew level with them, he called out, pointing towards Henrietta. He spoke Spanish, of course, but Uncle Loafy, as a sailor, had often been in Spanish-speaking countries and understood perfectly.

"Don't bother!" said the boy. "Those llamas don't like her."

"They'll get used to her," said Uncle Loafy, trying to sound cheerful.

The boy shook his head. "No, they won't, I'm afraid. They won't let her join them – I can tell you that."

Uncle Loafy frowned. "How can you be so sure?" he asked.

The boy smiled. "Because she's an alpaca, you see, and those others are all llamas."

Uncle Loafy's eyes widened. "You mean ..." he began.

"Yes," said the boy. "They look a bit the same, but there are differences. Alpacas are a bit smaller and they are much shyer. They're usually scared of llamas."

Uncle Loafy scratched his head. "I was pretty sure she was a llama," he said. "My friend Roger Porridge told me she was. At least, that's what I think he said."

Aunt Smiley was beginning to laugh. "You got it wrong, Loafy," she chided him. "You thought she was a llama, and all the time she was an alpaca."

Uncle Loafy looked very embarrassed. "I don't know all that much about animals," he said.

"So we see," said Aunt Smiley.

While all this was going on, nobody had paid much attention to Monkey Robertson, and now there seemed to be no sign of him.

"Do you think he's run away?" asked Noah.

"He'll be up to some mischief some-where or other," said Uncle Loafy. "That's what monkeys do, you know – they get up to mischief the moment you take your eyes off them."

He was right about that. Earlier that morning, when everybody was still zipped up in their tents, Monkey Robertson had decided to go off and explore their surroundings. There were some very interesting trees nearby, and he spent some time swinging about in these before he found himself on the edge of a small clearing. And there, in the clearing, was a small group of animals that looked rather like llamas, but were not quite the same.

Monkey Robertson could never resist the temptation to do something exciting, and now he decided that it would fun to ride on the smallest one of these llamas. And so he swung down from the trees, scampered across the clearing, and leaped on to the back of a very surprised llama. Then, pretending to be a jockey on a race horse, he dug his heels into the llama's sides, sending it helter-skelter down the path that led out of the clearing. As he did so, he whooped and chattered at the top of his voice, holding on to the llama's mane with one hand while waving the other in the air.

Alarmed by the monkey on her back, the little llama galloped off down the path and very soon came to the campsite, where Noah and Hatty were trying to soothe Henrietta after her unfortunate meeting with the unfriendly llamas.

The boy on the donkey gave a cry of surprise. "Look," he shouted. "That monkey has brought us an alpaca!"

Monkey Robertson brought his mount to a halt and jumped off.

"So this is an alpaca," said Uncle Loafy. "Now I see the difference."

The recently arrived alpaca was now looking at Henrietta, and advanced slowly to sniff at her nostrils.

"They like one another," whispered Hatty.

"Yes, they do," agreed Noah.

"Let's see what happens," said Aunt Smiley. "I think this is going to turn out well after all."

It did. Henrietta seemed very pleased with the company of a proper alpaca, and with a little whinny of farewell to her old friends, she started to trot back down the path with her new companion.

"Monkey Robertson saved the day!" exclaimed Uncle Loafy. "Now we can all go back to the boat."

They made their way back down the track to the bay where *The Ark* was anchored. Noah was sorry to say goodbye to Henrietta, but he realised that she was happier in freedom and with other creatures just like her. So that cheered him up.

Back on board, Uncle Loafy looked at his watch. "The tide will be going out soon," he said. "I think we should set off to our next destination."

"Where is that going to be?" asked Hatty.

"Australia," said Uncle Loafy. "Mrs Roo is itching to get back there."

"Are you sure she's a kangaroo?" asked Aunt Smiley, with a smile.

Uncle Loafy laughed. "I think so," he said. "But no doubt we shall find out once we get to Australia."

They set sail without further delay. Australia was a long way away, and they would have several weeks of sailing before they reached it. But already Noah and Hatty felt excited. They had never set foot in Australia, and they could hardly wait.

"I'm sure we'll find lots of kangaroos to adopt Mrs Roo," said Noah.

"I hope you're right," said Uncle Loafy. "Perhaps we'll find the rest of Mrs Roo's family. Old Grandma Roo, Aunt Roo, and all the little roo-let cousins. Maybe even Uncle Roo!"

~ 4 ~

The voyage from South America to Australia is a long one, across mile upon mile of wide and empty ocean. *The Ark*, though, was a strong boat, and Uncle Loafy was a good sailor. He knew exactly the right way to climb up a high wave and then slide down the other side, without any water getting over the side of the boat. He also knew how to work out where he was by looking up at the stars. There are no signposts in the sea, nor are there any hills or valleys to help you work out where you are. There are, of course, satellites that will give you your position, but Uncle Loafy was an old-fashioned sailor and he had not yet heard of satellites. "Nothing wrong with the stars," he was fond of saying. "That's why they're there, you know – to help us find our way."

They went through several storms on this voyage. The wind howled and the waves piled up like mountains, and at times everybody on board, except Uncle Loafy, rather wished they had never left dry land. Uncle Loafy did not think that. He seemed to enjoy a good storm, and stood on deck, steering the boat with a smile on his face, not at all worried about the soaking he was getting from the lashing rain, nor the blasts of wind that came at him from every direction.

"Check up on the animals, Noah," Uncle Loafy shouted in one such storm. "See that they're not getting too wet."

Noah made his way gingerly to the animals' cages towards the bow of the boat. They all looked miserable, and even Ram, who liked to bare his teeth and roar, seemed cowed by the heavy weather. Mrs Roo was not very happy either, and Monkey Robertson simply stared at Noah with a miserable look on his face.

"Don't worry," Noah shouted above

the noise of the storm. "Storms don't last forever."

He was right, of course, and a few hours later the clouds cleared, the sun came out and there, to everybody's delight, was the coast of Australia. It was still only a blue smudge on the horizon, but it was definitely Australia. That cheered everybody up, including the animals, who could smell land even before they could see it.

To celebrate the end of the storm and the sighting of land, Aunt Smiley made everybody a cup of hot chocolate, which Noah and Hatty drank while standing at the prow of the boat, looking out towards Australia. *In not much more than an hour,*

Noah thought, *I shall be standing on Australian soil for the first time*. It was a very exciting thought for him, as he had always longed to visit Australia.

And so had Monkey Robertson, it seemed. He had much less patience than Noah and Hatty, though, and as the boat came closer to land, he decided that he would be the first one on the beach. Looking about him to make sure that nobody was watching, the mischievous monkey leaped up on to the guard rail before diving down into the water and setting out for the beach with a strong breaststroke.

"Look at Monkey Robertson!" Hatty shouted. "He's jumped in."

Uncle Loafy was at the helm. He looked over in the direction Hatty was pointing, and shook his head. "That's extremely foolish," he said. "There are sharks about, and a monkey would make a very tasty morning snack for a shark."

No sooner had Uncle Loafy said this than Noah saw something in the water, not far from where Monkey Robertson was swimming. A dark triangular fin was circling in the water, getting closer to Monkey Robertson all the time.

"There's a shark!" Noah cried.

"Monkey Robertson will be eaten!" shouted Hatty. "Can't we do something to save him?"

It was Aunt Smiley who came to the rescue. Without losing any time, she rummaged in the picnic basket they were planning to take ashore. Taking out a large packet, she extracted from it ten or so tuna sandwiches that were going to be their lunch ashore. Now she flung these over the side of *The Ark,* right into the path of the circling shark. Monkey Robertson was still unaware of the danger in which he had landed himself, and was swimming towards the beach in an unconcerned fashion.

There is nothing a shark likes more than tuna sandwiches. Sensing the tuna in the water, the shark turned round, forgetting all about Monkey Robertson who, until that moment, had been its target. Now it darted about, collecting as many pieces of sandwich as it could manage.

Monkey Robertson reached the shore unharmed and looked very pleased with himself when everyone else eventually rowed ashore to join him. He was given a good telling-off by Uncle Loafy, but Noah

just gave Monkey Robertson a big hug. He was so relieved the monkey had survived – the boat would have been a much quieter, sadder place without him.

Noah had made a harness for Mrs Roo. The kangaroo did not seem to mind, and hopped beside them quite happily as they all made their way up the beach and into the forest beyond.

"Try to walk as quietly as you can," whispered Uncle Loafy. "If there are kangaroos about, we don't want to disturb them."

Treading very carefully, so as not to break any twigs or branches underfoot, they followed a path through the forest. Birds looked down at them from the trees above, sometimes fluttering up in squawking flocks, sometimes just watching in silence.

Noah found it rather eerie. He had that feeling that you sometimes get – that odd, hairs-on-the-back-of-your-neck feeling – that makes you think that somebody is watching you. Looking at his sister, he could see that Hatty had that feeling too, and he smiled at her to make her feel a little better.

Aunt Smiley saw this, and she smiled too, as she had been feeling a bit nervous herself, although she was not sure why. Perhaps it was the thought of snakes. She knew that there were dangerous snakes in Australia, and deadly spiders too. What if a snake – or a spider – was walking along the same path as they were and they suddenly came face to face with it? What then? Aunt Smiley did not like to think about it, and so she deliberately put all such thoughts out of her mind by thinking of things that had nothing to do with snakes or spiders. Or sharks, for that matter – she had not forgotten that there were some very large sharks in Australian waters. Although, now that they were on dry land, they did not need to worry about sharks. That did not stop you *thinking* about them, though ... and as she thought about great white sharks, she gave a little shiver.

Suddenly Uncle Loafy held up a hand to stop them. "There," he whispered, pointing in the direction of a clearing up ahead. "Look over there – a kangaroo."

The kangaroo was grazing on a patch of green grass in the middle of the clearing, unaware of being watched. Mrs Roo, watching the other kangaroo intently, gave an awkward little hop towards it. Hearing the sound, the kangaroo perked up its head and looked in their direction, its nose twitching inquisitively.

"He's seen us," said Aunt Smiley. "I hope he doesn't run away."

Hatty was about to point out that kangaroos never ran – they skipped – but she did not have the time to do this. The kangaroo suddenly gave a large bounce – much bigger than Mrs Roo's – not away from them, but towards them.

"He wants to get a better look at us," said Uncle Loafy.

The kangaroo had been staring at them intently. Suddenly it took another hop, and then one more, so that it stood within touching distance. And it was at this point that Noah slipped the harness off Mrs Roo.

What happened next was quite remarkable. The two kangaroos approached one another, touched noses as if to kiss, and

then started to dance. Noah and Hatty gasped in astonishment, while Aunt Smiley clapped her hands together in delight and Uncle Loafy whistled in admiration.

The two kangaroos finished their dance and then began to hop about together.

"He's teaching her!" exclaimed Aunt Smiley. "She's never been taught to bounce properly – now he's teaching her."

It was true. Since she had spent all her life in a zoo, Mrs Roo had never had the chance to learn how to be a proper kangaroo. Now the new friend was showing her how to hop like a kangaroo who had spent all her life in the Australian bush.

"She's picking it up quickly," said Noah. "Look at that."

Mrs Roo was a good learner. In captivity, her hops had been small ones – now she was bouncing higher and higher with every attempt. She was clearly enjoying it, and after a few more practice hops she bounced round the small group of astonished onlookers, just to show them what she could do.

Uncle Loafy looked at his watch. "We have to get back to the ship," he said. "The tide will be turning soon."

Noah found it sad to say goodbye to Mrs Roo, but he was pleased that she had found a friend. He was pleased, too, that this friend had accepted her so quickly and had proved to be a good teacher. That made it much easier to part and walk back to the ship.

As they made their way back down the

path, Hatty turned round to have one last look at the kangaroos. She stopped just in time, as they had hopped off into the undergrowth and she saw them only very briefly. Then they were gone – back in the place where they were meant to be, happy in their freedom.

"I think coming here was the right thing to do," she said to Uncle Loafy. "Mrs Roo seems very happy."

"Of course she is," said Uncle Loafy. "Wouldn't you be, if you were her?"

Hatty nodded. It was important, she thought, to imagine what it must be like to be somebody else – or even to be a kangaroo for that matter. It was difficult, though, to imagine what it must be like to be able to hop about like that. She wondered about that, and decided that it would undoubtedly be fun.

She thought about Ram and Monkey Robertson. Soon it would be their chance to be freed. It would be easy to let the monkey go free, she decided, but she was not sure about the tiger. How do you let go of a tiger whose main ambition is to eat you? She hoped that Uncle Loafy had a plan for that, because otherwise … Well, sometimes it's best not to think about these things.

~ 5 ~

India is a long way from Australia, but by running *The Ark*'s engine at full speed, and with a bit of wind behind them to push them along, in less than ten days they were within sight of the Indian coast. Cooking duties on board had been shared between the four of them, and on this leg of the trip it was Aunt Smiley's turn to prepare the meals.

"Since we're going to India," she said,

"we might as well get used to curries. They eat a lot of curries in India, you know."

Uncle Loafy thought this a very good idea. "I love hot food," he said. "Have you ever heard of the Scotch bonnet pepper?"

Nobody had, and they listened with interest as Uncle Loafy told them all about it.

"It is one of the hottest peppers there is," he said. "If you bite into a Scotch bonnet, oh my goodness, your mouth will catch fire."

"Then why do people eat them?" asked Hatty.

Uncle Loafy smiled. "That's the whole

point," he said. "They don't actually eat them. You put the pepper in the pot together with the rest of the food, but you fish it out just before you serve everybody. The Scotch bonnet adds spice to the stew, but the pepper itself is far too hot to put into your mouth."

"I shall not be using any Scotch bonnets," Aunt Smiley promised. "Just a little curry powder – that's all."

They enjoyed Aunt Smiley's curries. In particular, they liked the things that went with them – the sliced banana, the pieces of pineapple, the chopped coconut. Even Hatty, who had never liked spicy or hot food, was won round by Aunt

Smiley's creations, and said how she looked forward to the meals they would have in India.

Monkey Robertson often watched them eating their lunch. He was given a good supply of monkey food, but you could tell that he had his eyes on the dishes served up by Aunt Smiley. And one morning, a few days before they arrived in India, Monkey Robertson was to learn a rather hard lesson.

This is how it happened. Every morning after breakfast, Uncle Loafy would let Monkey Robertson out of his cage so that he could romp around the deck. The monkey liked to climb the mast and swing on the boat's aerial and flagstaff. He also liked to pull on any ropes that he found, and to generally interfere with whatever he could lay his hands on.

He enjoyed stealing food. If anybody was eating a banana while Monkey Robertson was on the loose, they had to be very careful indeed. If they left the banana unattended for more than a few moments, there would be a good chance that it would be snatched and eaten within minutes by Monkey Robertson. And the same went for chocolate, peanut butter sandwiches and cake of any description. Monkeys really enjoy all of those things and see no reason why they should not help themselves.

Monkey Robertson had no idea what curry tasted like. It looked rather good to him, with all its trimmings of sliced banana and coconut, and so one day, just when they were about to arrive on the Indian coast, he decided to help himself. Noah had left his lunch unattended for a few minutes, and Monkey Robertson saw his chance. Jumping down from the mast, he snatched Noah's plate and shovelled the food into his mouth.

Noah came back to discover that his lunch had been stolen. Looking about him, what he saw told him exactly what had happened. There was Monkey Robertson, jumping up and down, howling

at the top of his voice and pointing to his mouth.

"That's curry," Noah called out. "I could have warned you about that, Monkey Robertson!"

Noah did what he could to help.

Fetching a mug of water, he washed out the unfortunate monkey's mouth not once but several times. That helped, and after a while Monkey Robertson stopped screaming.

"Curry's hot," said Noah, as he handed Monkey Robertson a peeled banana to make him feel better. "I don't think monkeys like it."

And at that moment, there came that familiar cry.

"Land ahoy!" shouted Hatty from the bow.

In the excitement that followed, monkeys, and the problem they have with hot curry, were immediately forgotten.

Now there were more important things to do, including looking through the tele-scope to see if there was any suitable jungle on the coast. Suitable for what? For releasing a tiger, of course … And there was. Right ahead.

After *The Ark* had anchored in a bay that Uncle Loafy had decided was suitable, Ram's cage was lowered down into the shore boat. It was a tight fit, and the cage

was heavy, almost causing the small boat to sink. But it worked – just – and before too long, the party of Uncle Loafy, Aunt Smiley, Noah and Hatty was standing on the Indian beach, a growling tiger in the cage next to them.

"We'll drag the cage up to the top of the beach," said Uncle Loafy. "Then we'll let Ram go."

Noah frowned. He did not like to argue with his uncle, but it seemed to him that this plan might not work all that well.

"But what will happen when we open the door of the cage?" he asked. "What if the first thing that Ram does is to eat one of us?"

Uncle Loafy had not thought of that, but he quickly came up with a plan. There were several tall trees on the edge of the beach. They gave him an idea.

"We'll climb those trees," he said. "But we shall also tie a rope to the cage door. Then, when we are up a tree, we shall pull on the rope and open Ram's door. He'll come out, see the jungle, and run off into it." He smiled. "Simple, isn't it?"

"And we'll be safe?" asked Hatty, who was not sure that this was a particularly good plan.

"Yes," Uncle Loafy assured her. "Tigers can't climb trees, my dear – everybody knows that."

They dragged the cage up the beach. Ram did not like this, and let out several terrifying roars as his cage bumped over the sand. But soon they had each chosen a tree to climb and were safe in its higher branches.

"Ready?" asked Uncle Loafy.

"Yes!" they all shouted.

Uncle Loafy tugged at the rope and Ram's door sprung open. This surprised the tiger, who leaped out like a shot, growling fiercely as he did so.

And this was when Noah, and everybody else, discovered an interesting fact: tigers *can* climb trees.

~ 6 ~

Noah would never forget what happened next. As Ram bounded out of his cage, he looked about him, seemingly uncertain what to do. When he raised his head, though, and saw the people in the trees, he immediately made up his mind. It had been a long day so far and in the general excitement of reaching the Indian shore, nobody had remembered to give him his breakfast – or his lunch. Now, not all that far above his head, he could see a very tasty-looking meal looking down at him. That was Noah, who was hanging on to his branch as tightly as he possibly could.

Uttering a loud roar, Ram stood up on his two hind legs and locked his claws into Noah's tree. Then he began to pull himself up the tree trunk, all the while staring at Noah with steely eyes.

"Uncle Loafy!" shouted Noah. "You said tigers can't climb trees."

From the safety of his own tree, Uncle Loafy called out his reply. "Sorry," he shouted. "I was wrong. I *thought* they couldn't – but, you know, sometimes we get things wrong."

Noah closed his eyes. If he was going to be eaten by a tiger, then he thought that it might be best not to watch the whole business. But with his eyes closed, he did not see what happened next, which was something quite unexpected.

Monkey Robertson had been hiding in the small boat they had used to come

ashore. Now, seeing what was happening, he dashed out and scampered up to Ram, just out of reach, but close enough to attract the tiger's attention. Seeing the monkey, the tiger gave a warning growl, as if to say: *Don't bother me right now – I'm having my lunch.* And then he sniffed.

Tigers like curry. That is a little-known fact, but there's nothing a tiger likes more than a spot of curry, and when Ram smelt the curry that was still on the fur around Monkey Robertson's mouth, he was distracted from his plan to eat Noah. Curried monkey, he thought, would be an even tastier snack than a boy, and he could always have the boy as his second course.

Ram let go of the tree trunk and landed on the ground below, rather close to Monkey Robertson. But the monkey was prepared for this, and scampered off towards the jungle. Ram pursued him, completely forgetting about the people up the trees. This gave them the chance to climb down as quickly as they could and run back to the boat at the bottom of the beach. Meanwhile, Monkey Robertson had led the furious tiger into the jungle. And there he was able to find a suitable vine to swing on, well out of reach of the snarling tiger below.

Somebody was watching this, and this somebody was a large and very beautiful

tiger, who had been prowling round the jungle looking for a suitable friend. When she saw Ram, she gave him a welcoming growl. This was quite enough for him to lose interest in the annoying monkey on the vine, and to go over and introduce himself.

They became friends immediately, and without so much as a final glance at Monkey Robertson, Ram walked off into the jungle with the other tiger. He was very pleased with the jungle, which struck him as being an ideal home for a stripy creature like himself, and he was pleased, too, with his new companion. Perhaps they would have a few tiger cubs together and look after this piece of jungle. Those were the thoughts going through his mind as he disappeared into the undergrowth beneath the trees. He was no longer growling, but purring, in the loud way in which tigers do. And his new friend was purring too, and so everybody was happy.

Monkey Robertson galloped back to the boat, where he was given a hero's welcome.

"You saved my life," cried Noah as he handed the monkey a banana. "You are a real hero, Monkey Robertson."

Monkey Robertson stuffed the whole banana into his mouth. Monkeys do not have good table manners, but that was the last thing that mattered on the trip back to *The Ark*. What mattered was they were all safe, Ram was happy in his new home, and they could now leave for Africa, and the final part of *The Ark*'s mission. That would be exciting too, but in a very different way, as we shall shortly see.

~ 7 ~

*T*he *Ark* sailed west towards Africa. The weather was gentle, and there were few big waves, only a low swell. Noah and Hatty enjoyed the voyage, watching the sea go by, and sitting in the sun under the wide-brimmed sun hats that Aunt Smiley had made for them out of an old sail. Monkey Robertson often sat beside them, staring out at the sea, thinking monkey thoughts, while Uncle Loafy and

Aunt Smiley played cards under the shade of a deck umbrella.

It was Noah's turn to cook on this part of the voyage, and he spent long hours in the galley, making delicious meals. In this task he was helped by Monkey Robertson, who proved to be a rather good cook, helping with the chopping up of vegetables and the peeling of fruit, much of which he would eat himself if Noah was not looking at the time.

Everybody was enjoying themselves so much on this lazy voyage that it was almost a disappointment to see Africa appear on the horizon. But, as Uncle Loafy pointed out, they had a job to do, and they could not stay at sea forever. So, once *The Ark* was safely anchored, they all climbed into a small boat and rowed ashore. Monkey Robertson was excited, as he knew that he would soon find other monkeys, but Noah and Hatty sensed that he was also feeling a bit sad. This was where they would be leaving him – and he knew that. It is not easy to leave your friends, especially if you have had all sorts of adventures with them.

The beach on which they landed was quite deserted. This was a bit surprising, as the sand was clean and the water of the bay was bright and warm.

"You'd think that there would be

people around," said Hatty. "You'd think that this would be a good place to swim."

"Or to have a picnic," said Noah.

Uncle Loafy frowned and sniffed the air. "I'm not sure about this place," he said. "There's something wrong, if you ask me."

But he could not think of what that might be, and before he had the chance to say anything more, Noah was pointing excitedly to one of the palm trees on the edge of the sand.

"Over there!" he said. "Look!"

They all looked in the direction in which Noah was pointing. There, at the top of one of the trees, was a family of

monkeys, staring down at their visitors,
chattering amongst themselves.

Monkey Robertson saw them too, and
he scampered across the sand towards
the tree. Then, without any hesitation, he
climbed up the tree to join the group above

him. They gave him a loud welcome, reaching out to touch him and stroke his fur.

"It looks like we've come to the right place," said Aunt Smiley, smiling with pleasure. "I think Monkey Robertson is going to be very happy."

"We should leave him," said Uncle Loafy. "He's found his new family now."

Noah and Hatty waved to Monkey Robertson, and he waved back. For a few moments it looked as if he was going to follow them as they began to walk back to their boat, but his new family seemed unwilling to let him go.

"He'll be happy here," said Uncle Loafy. "Come along, everyone."

They rowed back out to *The Ark*, and set about getting the ship ready to leave. There was a lot to do — sails to prepare, ropes to unwind, and decks to be tidied. It was while they were doing these tasks that they suddenly realised what Uncle Loafy had smelt on the wind. Trouble!

They arrived quite suddenly. One moment there was nobody about, and then a small boat, painted black and flying the pirate flag — the skull and crossbones — came into sight round a headland. This boat made straight for them and, before they could do anything about it, had tied itself up alongside *The Ark*. Then, without so much as a by-your-leave, a group of tough-looking men and women climbed on to the deck.

"Pirates!" whispered Noah under his breath.

They were not nice pirates. In fact, they were rather unpleasant pirates, who jumped on board and immediately tied everybody up. Then they went into the ship's galley and took out all the food, which they set out on the deck as a great feast for themselves. While they were doing this, the whole crew of *The Ark* looked on, their hands tied behind their backs, all wondering and dreading what might happen next.

The pirates had brought sacks with

them, and they now began to explore *The Ark,* taking anything of value on which they could lay their hands. Noah saw his favourite penknife disappear into a pirate's pocket, and Hatty watched as the head pirate guzzled down every last chocolate from a box of chocolates she had been given. In addition, they took all the honey, jam and crisps that they could find in the kitchen.

It all looked rather hopeless for the Wilds. But then, out of the corner of his eye, Noah saw something swimming in the water. At first he thought it must be a seal, but after a moment or two he realised that it was something quite different.

Straining his eyes, he saw that it was Monkey Robertson.

Something inside him told Noah that he should not give the pirates any warning of Monkey Robertson's approach. So Noah looked in the opposite direction, with the result that none of the pirates saw Monkey Robertson climb up on to the boat they had used to come out to *The Ark*. Nor did they see him deftly untie the knot in the rope that kept the pirate boat attached to *The Ark*. And they certainly did not see him as he leaped lightly up on to the deck of *The Ark* and crept up behind the Wild family to untie the knots that bound their hands.

Suddenly one of the pirates gave a cry. "Our boat!" he shouted. "It's beginning to drift away."

This was the signal for the pirates to rush across the deck and jump into the now detached boat. Once on board, they struggled to get the engine going but failed. This was because Monkey Robertson, who was a very intelligent monkey, had taken the key.

The pirate boat drifted away, the pirates shouting angrily but unable to do anything about it. As they fumed and fretted, Uncle Loafy went to the radio and sent an urgent message to the local police. "If you'd like to catch a boatload of desperate pirates," he said, "you'll see them floating about in the bay."

That done, Uncle Loafy thanked Monkey Robertson for his help, gave him a whole bunch of bananas, and then said he supposed it was time for them to take

him back to his new friends on the shore. The monkey, however, had other ideas. When Uncle Loafy pointed to the shore and asked him if he was ready to return, Monkey Robertson immediately climbed up the mast, as high as he could. There, sitting on a spar, he shook his head vehemently, making it quite clear that he wanted to stay with his friends on *The Ark*.

Noah and Hatty pleaded with Uncle Loafy to let Monkey Robertson stay. "He won't be any trouble," said Hatty. "I'm sure he'll promise to be good."

It was as if Monkey Robertson understood exactly what she said, as he nodded his head furiously.

Uncle Loafy looked doubtful. "It would be better for him to live with other monkeys," he said.

Noah begged him to reconsider. "He obviously wants to be with us," he said. "And surely we should let him do what he wants to do. That's the reason why we freed the animals in the first place, wasn't it?"

Uncle Loafy thought for a moment. He looked at Aunt Smiley, who looked back at him.

"I think Noah's right," she said at last. "I think that's what Monkey Robertson wants."

"In that case," said Uncle Loafy, "he can stay on board. He'll be useful in getting the sails up – he scampers up the mast far more quickly than any of us."

They set out to sea a few hours later. Monkey Robertson seemed very grateful to be allowed to stay, and was very helpful in every way. He was now becoming very good at chopping up vegetables and stirring soup, and he was also learning to wash up.

The journey took a long time, but at last they were in sight of *The Ark*'s home port and preparing to pack their kitbags. Uncle Loafy came back with them to the house, as did Monkey Robertson, who was on his best behaviour. And there, on the doormat, was a letter from their parents. They were coming home, they said, because they had had enough of climbing mountains. They would look around for a new job, they said, and they hoped they would find one.

"They need look no further," said Uncle Loafy. "I have decided to use *The Ark* to take people for short trips out to sea. I'll need crew — as well as Monkey Robertson, of course."

"I think they'll like that," said Aunt Smiley. "I shall write to them this very day."

And she did. And they wrote back to say that they would be overjoyed to take up Uncle Loafy's offer of a job on *The Ark*. Would it be possible, they asked, for them all to live together once they were back? That would mean Aunt Smiley could look after Noah and Hatty while they were off at sea with Uncle Loafy and Monkey Robertson.

"Oh, please say yes, Aunt Smiley," urged Noah. "Then you can look after me and Hatty while everyone's at sea."

Aunt Smiley did not hesitate. "That would make me very happy," she said, and smiled.

Then Noah remembered there was something he needed to ask. "And would that make YOU happy, Monkey

Robertson?" he asked. "Working on the boat, and living with us at the weekend?"

And Monkey Robertson leaped on to Noah's shoulder, ate a whole banana in one gulp, and nodded his head twenty-seven times in a row.

Have you read these amazing stories by **Alexander McCall Smith?**